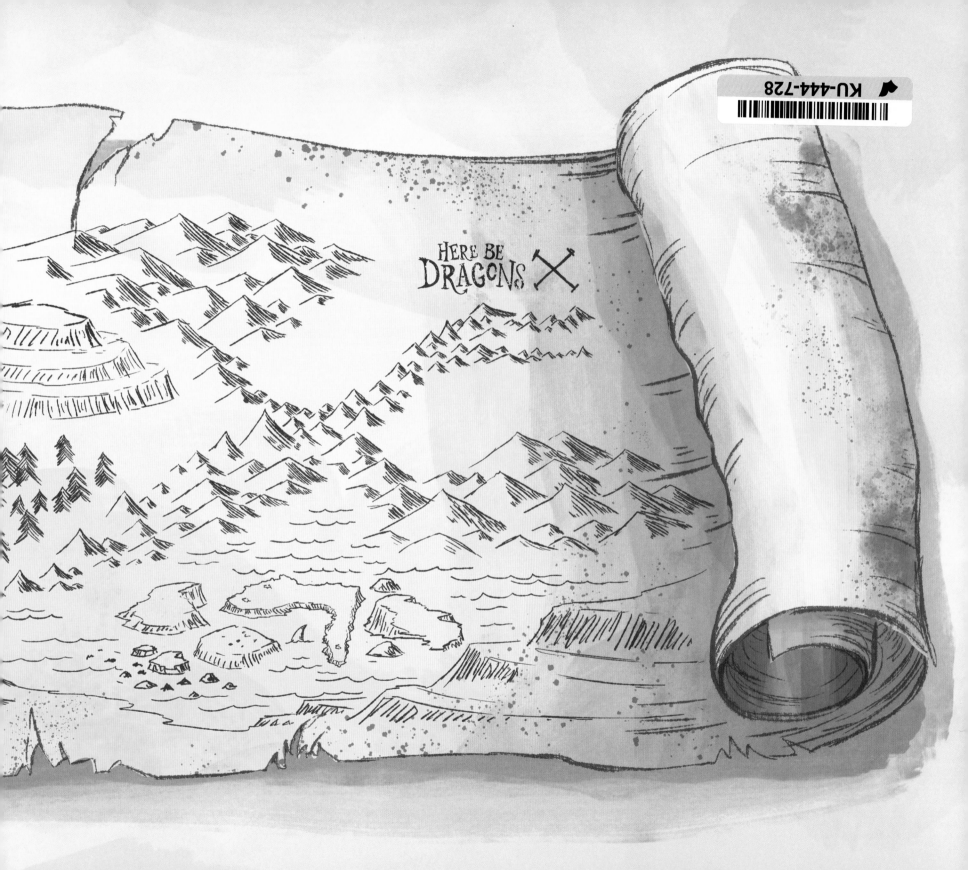

HERE BE
DRAGONS ✗

For Ilona — S.L.

For Hanne, who wouldn't be at all happy about all
this dragon slaying — P.D.

Text © 2021 Susannah Lloyd. Illustrations © 2021 Paddy Donnelly.
First published in 2021 by Frances Lincoln Children's Books, an imprint of The Quarto Group,
The Old Brewery, 6 Blundell Street, London N7 9BH, United Kingdom.
T (0)20 7700 6700 F (0)20 7700 8066 www.QuartoKnows.com
A catalogue record for this book is available from the British Library.
ISBN 978-0-7112-5661-3
The illustrations were created digitally
Set in Old Claude LP
Published and edited by Katie Cotton
Designed by Zoë Tucker
Production by Dawn Cameron
Manufactured in Guangdong, China CC 102020

HAPPY READING!

PADDY
DONNELLY

2021

SUSANNAH LLOYD   PADDY DONNELLY

HERE BE
DRAGONS

Frances Lincoln
Children's Books

YE MAGICAL POTION*, TURNS LUMPS OF COAL INTO ~~MORE LUMPS OF COAL~~ GOLD (1.5% GUARANTEED TO WORK, OR YOUR MONEY BACK)

Ye Olde SHOPPE *for the Gullible and Rich*

ALL POTIONS SHOULD ONLY BE USED UNDER THE SUPERVISION OF A QUALIFIED AND RESPONSIBLE WIZARD

Lancelot

THE ART OF WOOING HOW AND WHO TO WOO. A KNIGHT'S GUIDE TO DAMSELS. REFUNDS ARE NOT ACCEPTED.

'GENUINE' DRAGON MAPS

You'll never guess what the other knights said. "There's no such thing as a dragon." I said, "Forsooth! There is TOO such a thing!" And I'm gonna find one. AND battle it. So there! HUZZAH! You only have to know where to look. And I do know where. I have a map, and it says…

Today's Specials

GOBLIN REMOVER, 100 DOUBLOONS. *YOU MUST SUPPLY YOUR OWN GOBLIN.

GRIFFIN EGGS. (SHATTERPROOF. BUY 2 GET A 3RD HALF PRICE)

MAGICAL FAIRIE DUST (* MAY CONTAIN NUTS)

COURT JESTER, SLIGHTLY USED.

SPARE LUTES

BARGAINS!

"Verily, you will not find one," the other knights said.

They never believe me. Well, what do they know?!

Right. Things to look out for...
Treasure, it says here.
'Dragons like to hoard treasure.'
Shiny, sparkly treasure.

Shouldn't be
too hard to spot...

There ist not a single bit of treasure in these dashed woods. Ah, well.

What's next?

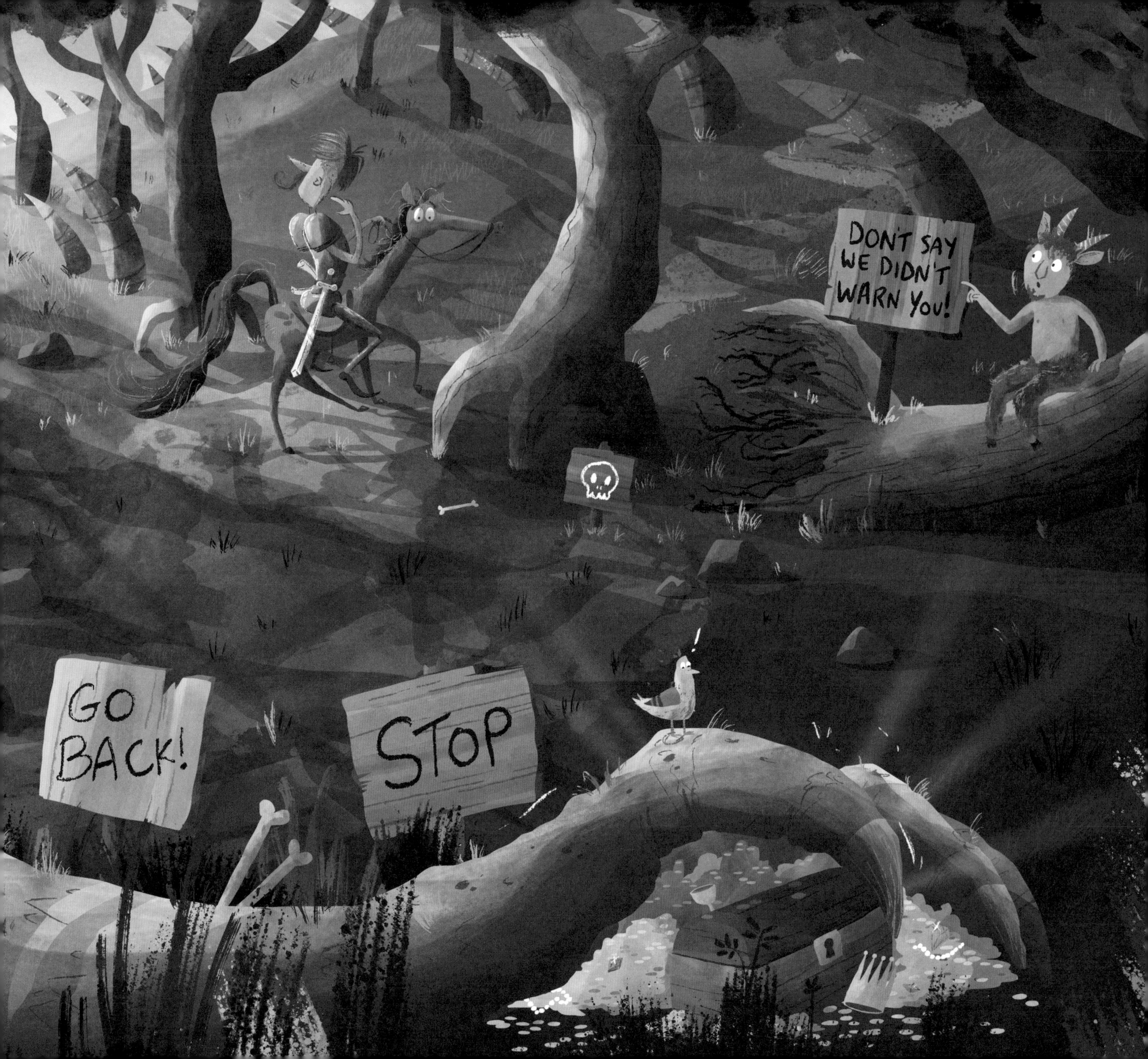
DON'T SAY WE DIDN'T WARN YOU!
GO BACK!
STOP

Ah, yes. 'Failing that, you can
usually tell if a dragon's nearby
from the burnt remains
of its dinner.'

By my liege,
I wonder what they eat?

Not that I'll be able to
see it, with all this mess
around here.

Someone should
really clear up, once in a while.

Perchance t'will be
a dragon in this burrow?

Even just a *little* one?

Egads!
I'm starting to
wonder if I'll ever
find one.

Oh, hello there! Perhaps you can help me.
It says in my map, 'A sure sign of a dragon is
a DAMSEL-IN-DISTRESS, usually a high-
born lady, perhaps a princess... pointy hat and
whatnot... almost always tied to something so
she can't escape.' Mmmm...

I don't suppose you
have seen anything
like that?

No?
How about dragons?
Seen any dragons?

I'm sorry my dear,
I really can't understand
what you're saying.

Verily, if you want
to tell me something
then you should
really take that silly
handkerchief out of
your mouth.

But look yonder!
A cave. Dragons
love caves!

Now there's no need to panic, my dear.
I know that caves can be rather
alarming. But I am a brave
and fearless knight and
I am going to find
myself a
dragon.

Right now!

Tis a bit dark in here,
methinks. Cannot
see a thing!

Ouch!
That hurt!

Dashed pointy thing
got me right on
the bottom!

Who ist mucking about with arrows out there?
I bet it was that foolish maiden. Someone could get hurt, verily!

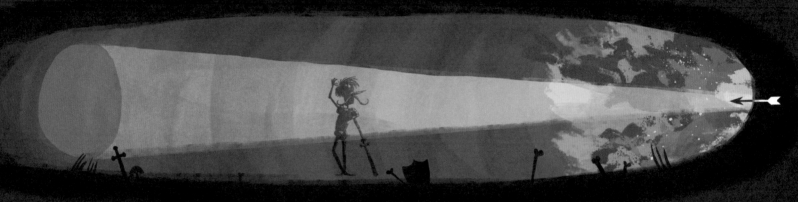

Is it just me or is it getting hot in here? Quite toasty!

Prithee now, which way is out? Ah! This way. Tum tee tum.

Woah, there!

Bit steep, eh what?

No wonder I couldn't see-eth where I was going!
It's all this blasted **smoke.** Shouldst be a rule
against starting fires down there.
Just look at my map. Tis ruined!

And not one dragon.
Egads!

Maybe the other knights were right. Maybe there really is no such thing as a dragon.

I might just *tell* them I saw a dragon anyway.

They'll never need to know.

Prithee, has anyone
seen my dashed horse?